AF427969

SEVEN MINUTES AWAY FROM A SLOCOMB TOMATO

SEVEN MINUTES FROM A SLOCOMB TOMATO

Cover Design by Tommy Adkins
and Deb Gabel

Published by ASODA and Amazon
Printed in the USA
Editor: Deb Gabel

https://www.amazon.com/Tommy-Adkins/e/B07C1XC1W2/ref=aufs_dp_fta_dsk

For THE PUPPETS

Our first gig was in Hartford,

Battle of the Bands.

(that's you too, Gerry)

Other Books by Tommy Adkins

Taters, Maters with Rice and Beans

Spinning Words

Blue Plate Special

Golden Isle
Join Our Golden Isle Facebook Page

Jim and Rose

The Katy Ann

Three Quarters Past a Lifetime

Sara's Italian Haunt

Apple Bay

Lloyd and the Wolf

Jeremiah Stone

Southern Folk Tales for the Holidays

Danny Right

SEVEN MINUTES AWAY

FROM A

SLOCOMB TOMATO

1

Junior Barns and Butch, his companion, a 55 pound brown, black, orange and white mixture of maybe 5 kinds of mongrels, stood halfway up the hill from the Barns' lake and the old Barns home site. A four bedroom brick home was still there but that was empty now.

Hot, dang! Hot middle of July. Junior pulled his t-shirt up over his belly and wiped sweat from his forehead and eyes. He looked down at Butch, a half-pound of tongue hanging out the side of his mouth, saliva dripping to the ground. They both looked up at Barns' drive. A path ran from the highway down behind the house and back up to the Enterprise Highway. There sat a brand spanking new '75 Ford Granada. Baby blue with a landau roof. It gleamed in the sunlight but Junior could tell it was cool as a cucumber inside. Dark windows and a/c took care of that.

Junior Barns was the last remaining Barns. All of this was his now. One hundred and fifty acres. The house sat by a small lake. Behind the lake about a quarter mile, a log cabin. A quarter mile behind the cabin, a barn with an old John Deere and a '69 Chevy pick-up. Half a mile behind the cabin back in the woods, a shack. Most of the money that was in the Daleville Bank and this old dog all belonged to Junior. Thirty five years old, almost six foot, long hair tied into a pony tail. He did not even own a pair of long pants. What Junior did have, it seems, was an abundance of common sense. Even though he didn't look it.

The Ford pulled to a stop. She stepped out. Black business suit. Skirt cut at the knees. Toes just showing on her four inch heels.

Shoes not made for walking in dirt. She
pulled her jacket off and tossed it into the
car. Her bare arms showed in her satin
white top. Arms almost muscular, she had
lifted weights at some point. Blond hair, a
butch cut, short. Dark expensive sun
glasses. She stepped around in front of the
car, keeping her balance with her right hand
on the hood of the car.
"Junior, Junior Barns?"
Junior raised his hand up to block out the
sun.
"Yes ma'am. That's me."
"Could we talk?"
Junior stared at her for a couple of seconds.
"Well sure, I reckon. How 'bout up at the
diner on the highway. I could use a sweet
tea, maybe some pie."
"Jump in the car. I'll drive."
She climbed back in the car. Junior looked
down at Butch.
"You go on back to the house now."
Butch pulled his tongue back into his
mouth and trotted down the hill to the

cabin. Junior walked up the hill and climbed into the Ford. It was cool inside, almost cold. She pulled the shift down into 'drive' and they rolled around the path up to the highway. She took a right and half a mile down on the left, they came to the diner. It still resembled the old convenience store it used to be...only the aromas coming from it now made the mouth water.

Inside, booths ringed the outer wall and there was a counter with stools in the center.

They sat in the first booth by the door. Only one other customer was parked at the bar halfway down. An old fellow with a USPS shirt on, sipping coffee. Sylvia met them at the table with menus. Junior ordered tea, the lady ordered a Pepsi. Sylvia let her know they only had Coke. The lady said that would be fine.

The lady reached over and pulled a pad and pen from her purse, but before she could start her conversation, Sylvia was back with their drinks.

"Junior, you gonna have the apple pie?"

"Yes ma'am. I think so."

"Cheese or ice cream?"

"Just straight up today, I think."

"And you, ma'am?"

The lady looked up at Sylvia, maybe a little disturbed. "No, no. I'm fine."

Junior stopped Sylvia before she could turn away.

"Are you sure? I mean, this is the best apple pie in Alabama, maybe the south!"

The lady smiled politely but before she could say anything, Junior did.

"Sylvia, bring her a piece with cheese. If she don't eat it, then I'll take it home. Me or Butch will take care of it."

Sylvia, a big grin on her face said,

"Yes sir Mr. Junior, you got it."

She turned and walked away.

The lady gave Junior a warm smile with
cold eyes. A talent she had.

The old man at the bar stood, reached in his
pocket, pulled out a little folding money
and left three dollars by his coffee cup. He
started for the door but stopped and looked
back.
"Say Junior, what kinda mood is JW in
today? I got a registered letter for him and
I hate to get run off, with him naked and an
ax in his hand."
Junior smiled.
"I'll be at the cabin this afternoon. Just
come on by and I'll walk down to the shack
with you."
The old man saluted and walked on out the
door. Sylvia returned to the table with two
slices of pie. One with cheese, one
without. She gave Junior a wink, flirting
with him less than normal because he was
with a lady.

Junior took a sip of his tea and dug into his

pie.

"Go ahead Miss...uh.. I don't even know your name."

"Glenda Wells. I represent the Morgan and Sims company out of Atlanta, GA."

Junior looked up from his pie.

"I know Atlanta. Been there a couple times. Sure wouldn't want to live there. I have wondered how anybody gets around in that mess."

"Mr. Barns, Morgan and Sims are very interested in your property."

"How so, Miss Glenda?"

Junior took a large bite of pie.

She paused for a second, not sure how she appreciated the Miss Glenda reference.

"They could be very interested in purchasing your land. Their pockets are very deep, Mr. Barns."

"Oh, Miss Glenda. My pockets are kinda deep too. Besides, my land ain't for sale."

"Mr. Barns could we talk this over a few drinks and dinner tonight."

Junior took the last bite of his pie and
washed it down with tea.
"Well, I've already got dinner plans, but I'll
be sipping a little Jim Bean on the porch
tonight if you would like to join me."
"I would love to."

Junior got up and threw a twenty on the
table.
"If you don't mind, Miss Glenda, I think
I'd like to walk home."
He looked back over his shoulder just as
the lady took a bite of the pie. Junior
stopped at the end of the counter where the
cash register was by the door. He pulled
some money from his shorts pocket and
paid the ticket. Sylvia smiled, winked
again.
"You come back soon, Junior."

Junior smiled back and noticed another
button was undone on Sylvia's uniform.
Couldn't nobody help but notice that.

2

Junior spent the afternoon cooking a pot of turnip greens with a chunk of bacon and a pot of northern beans with bell pepper, jalapeños along with enough Cajun seasoning and hot sauce to make a coonass turn around. A pan of cornbread and a fresh sliced Vidalia from Georgia. And tomatoes from over in Slocomb.

Junior took a tray with some of each down to the shack and pounded on the door. He left the tray along with the registered letter, that Postman Bob was to afraid to deliver, on the porch for JW.

From the porch of Junior's cabin in one of the two rocking chairs, you could see the lake. Sparkling water with an occasional turtle poking his head up. After sunset, you could hear the tree frogs and the crickets. He sat, rocked and sipped on two fingers of Crown. He called all whiskey Jim Beam. Something he got from his mother-in-law way back. Finally the summer day was giving way to a cool breeze across the lake.

He could see the headlights pulling off the highway down the path and a car stopping. The lights went out and the interior door light of the Ford opened and closed. Glenda Wells stepped out of the Granada, this time more prepared. She wore sandals, tight blue jeans and a red and black flannel shirt unbuttoned and tied at the bottom. She bounced down the slight grade to Junior's porch.
"Such a beautiful setting, Mr. Barns!"
"Why don't you just make it Junior, Miss Glenda. Come on up. This chair is waiting just for you."
"Why don't you just make it Glenda."
She stepped up on the porch and took a seat

in the empty rocker.

"How about a sip of Crown."

"I believe I will, Junior," she said with a smile. "I though you said Jim Beam?"

"Well, tonight, Jim turned into Crown."

He stepped inside and poured a double into a whiskey glass with one ice cube. Back out on the porch:

"Enjoy. There is plenty more where that came from."

"I can certainly understand why you wouldn't want to sell this place. The view, the sweet smell of this clean air."

"Yes, ma'am, some of the many reasons."

He took a sip. She took a sip.

"So tell me about this fellow that runs around naked and chases people with an ax."

"Got to tell you. That tale has been greatly exaggerated. I don't think I've ever seen him with an ax."

They both laughed and then sat silent for a few minutes. The tree frogs filled in the pause in conversation.

Junior thought *'this lady has changed her overall attitude. Maybe she has just slowed down or maybe it's a new angle on her bid to buying his property. Either way, it was better'*.

"Can I ask you what the JW stands for?"
Junior took another sip and looked over at her.
"Sure. John Wayne."
They both laughed until tears came.

A spell went by in silence, and then maybe an hour of small talk.
"How about another splash?"
She put her hand over the glass.
"No, no. I really have to go."
She sat the glass down on the little table between the two chairs and stood. She made eye contact with Junior and he understood it as, *I would love to stay the night.* However, she stepped down off the

porch. He stood and called out to her.
"How 'bout lunch tomorrow?"
She turned. "OK."
Junior smiled.
"I'll pick you up about eleven. Daleville
Inn, right?"
"Make it eleven thirty. I'll be out front."
 And she walked up the path around the
lake and up to the Ford. The lights came
on and it pulled around to the highway.

Junior walked up to the lake and out onto
the pier, a sturdy wooden structure built by
Junior and JW. Fifteen feet out into the
small lake. The lake was crystal clean
although it had some turtles, some frogs
and some nice-sized fish.

Junior dropped his shorts, pulled off his t-
shirt and dove in. The cool water,
moonlight and fresh air cleared his head for
a sweet dream sleep.

3

At exactly eleven thirty, a '69 Chevy pick-up, blue and white but mostly rust pulled up to the entrance of the Daleville Inn. Glenda Wells stood on the curb, this time wearing cut-off jean shorts, an Atlanta Braves t-shirt and flip flops. Junior pulled to a stop, got out and opened the passenger door.
"You like seafood?"
"Love it," she said as she climbed in. They pulled out onto 85, took a right and drove not too far to Lynns Seafood Cafe.

They had the catfish, fries, slaw, hushpuppies, pickles and onion. Sweet tea. She said she had never had anything better in her whole life.

Junior drove them back around to his cabin. She asked about the field of pine trees behind his cabin and where the shack was.

12.5

He explained that his great-granddad had brought seedligs back from Georgia and planted them in the big empty field. The shack was set a hundred feet back in the field and on a half-acre clearing. He eased the pick-up down the drive to the barn but stopped short by the lake. They walked out on the dock to the end. He sat down dangling his feet over the edge.
"Too bad you didn't bring a swimsuit."
She pulled her shorts off sporting tiny yellow panties.
"I'm good. I just don't have a top."
Junior stood up and stepped out of his flip flops, pulled off his t-shirt, stepped out of his shorts and dove into the lake. She pulled off her t-shirt and dove in after him. The swim was refreshing but innocent.

Back at the cabin, they sat on the porch wrapped in towels and drinking freshly made lemonade. The noonday sun was past now and heading to sinking in the west.

Butch joined them on the porch after a day
spent with J W. He laid at the edge of the
steps and fell asleep. Junior leaned forward
in his chair.
"You want to stay the night?"
"I thought you would never ask!"

Junior tightened his towel and walked
inside. Butch followed and Junior
refreshed his water dish, then scooped
some food into his bowl. He returned to
the porch with a tray of ham and swiss
sandwiches on rye with slices of tomato. A
few sports peppers and slices of dill
pickles. He sat the tray on the table
between the two chairs.
"Wine?"
"How about White Zin with ice?"
He frowned. "Somehow I knew that."
Back out on the porch with a stemmed
glass of white wine and another glass of ice
along with a glass of Cab for him. They
scarfed the sandwiches down and sat back
sipping on the wine.

"You want to tell me about John Wayne?"
"I could, but it's a long story."
"We got wine?"
"Plenty."
"Then let's hear it."
They both took sips at the same time and it struck them funny. Finally the laughter subsided.

"First of all, JW is a white guy a little older than me. Probably forty-two or three. Six foot tall in fairly good shape. Strong as an ox. He picked up telephone pole-sized posts that we used for the pier like they were nothing. Whether he is crazy or not, not my call. One day he has a beard, the next day not. Hair always long, brown with a little gray. I met him at the Daleville Inn bar one night. He wandered in and sat beside me on a bar stool. Said he was there to hear a local band from Dothan."
"I know Dothan! I flew into Dothan and rented a car."
"A great little town. I lived there for a

while myself. Anyway, the night moved
on, the band played and were really good.
JW bragged on them, flirted with a good-
looking long-haired waitress, then asked
me if I knew a good place to stay for the
night. I told him the inn was good as any.
He told me he was a little short on change.
I thought a minute, then offered him the
shack. I told him one room and a bath.
That was about seven years ago. JW it
turns out writes lyrics and sends them to a
fellow in Atlanta who puts them to music.
Various artists record them and lo in
behold, most of them are hits. The
registered letters he gets are royalty checks
enough to buy Alabama. He sends money
out to good causes, then he's broke again.
He does spend most of his time naked but
he don't chase folks with an ax."
She held out her glass.
"Do you have more wine?"
Junior stood up. "Of course."
"Hey, I got to tell you. I never heard of a

hit song written by John Wayne.”
“Well, it seems part of the deal is the artist
gets to claim the song.”
“That’s a shame.”

Junior refilled their glasses and brought a
fresh glass of ice. She filled her wine glass
with ice.
“You sure you don’t want to sell this place?
You could do a lot with that much money.”
“I think I told you before, I have lots of
money. You know folks have different
wants and needs. They have different ideas
of what a successful life is. Some need to
run companies, some need to write books,
some need to have families, fix things,
plant seeds and grow things. Me... I kinda
like sitting on the porch. Listening to the
tree frogs, breathing the fresh air, thinking
about and realizing there is a God. I’m at
home here, Glenda. I do my best to take
care of JW and Butch. I leave big tips and
pass money around to folks who need it. I

try my best to turn my back on hate and
focus on good. You know, in this old world
full of opinion, all we really need is love.
It's a full-time job and I think I do it best
right here."

It was late. She stood and let her towel
drop to the floor. She reached out her hand
and he took it. She lead him inside to the
bedroom. A large room. A queen-sized bed
built from heavy timber. A dark brown
spread with tan sheets. One chest of
drawers. Two bedside tables. A large
window next to the bed. A door leading to
a very large bath. They crawled into bed
and held each other close. Butch joined
them and curled up on the rug by the bed.
She pulled his arm over her and whispered,
"I do love the pine trees. They are so
green."

They all closed their eyes and fell into
heavy sleep.

4

Junior woke to the front door closing. He thought he was still holding Glenda but it turned out to be a pillow with a note on it.

Junior, I have to catch the 8 o'clock plane out of Dothan to Atlanta. I have to get back to the office and explain that you do not want to sell your land. Loved our time together and hope we will meet again. Give my regards to JW and pet Butch on the head.
Glenda

Junior slipped out of bed and halfway through brushing his teeth, he realized he needed to see her before she left. He pulled on shorts, a t-shirt and slipped on Crocs. He wrote a note and wrapped it around Butch's collar for JW to take care of him.

The old pick-up came to life and he hit the
highway, turning left on 84 and let her roll.
He arrived at the Dothan airport at 8:10 and
was told the 8 o'clock to Atlanta had just
left.
"When's the next flight?"
"You're in luck. It's at 8:30 and there is
one seat left."
Junior reached into his pocket, pulled out
his wallet and Master Card and threw it on
the counter. The lady handed him a ticket.
"You can go ahead and check your baggage
in now."
"I don't have any."
She looked at him funny.
"Then you can take a seat. Your flight will
be ready shortly."

Somewhere over Columbus, Georgia,
Glenda thought of Junior, JW, Butch, the
pines and the cabin. She knew this was
part of her life she would never forget. She
leaned back in her seat and let the roar of
the engines lull her to sleep.

Junior sat in the airport terminal wondering if he was doing the right thing. Maybe this is just what she had in mind. Get him to the big city and try and make the hard sell. Oh well. He had been to Atlanta once and best he could remember he hated it. This would give him a chance to confirm that.

The rough touch of the wheels on the Hartsfield runway woke Glenda. She stretched and filed down the aisle, out of the plane and through her gate.

On the 65th floor of the high rise on Decatur Street, she stood in the offices of Morgan and Sims Company. Donald Webb held out his hand.
"Welcome back, Glenda! I hope your trip went well. Why don't you step into my office and bring me up to speed."
Glenda was back in her business clothes: black skirt and jacket, along with a white shirt. High-heeled pumps with no stockings on her almost perfect legs.

"Well, mostly what I have to report is Mr.
Barns doesn't want to sell. He seems very
adamant about the fact that he is right
where he is supposed to be."
Donald Webb walked around behind his
desk and sat in the plush high back leather
chair.
"Glenda would you care for a drink?"
"No sir, I'm good."
"You're not giving up, are you? This
would be one of the largest commission
pay-offs in the history of this company."
"Oh no, sir. If my intuition is right and it
usually is, Mr. Barns is crawling into a cab
right now here in Atlanta heading our way."

Junior stepped from the plane out of the
gate and stopped at the first ATM. He
swiped his card and drew out a hundred
dollars twice. Down the escalator, through
the automatic doors and out on the street,
he hailed a cab to the Morgan and Sims
Company.

Webb leaned back in his chair.

"So, if you are right, why don't you take a couple of days and show Mr. Barns the best of Atlanta? Maybe you can change his mind."

"That's my plan."

Junior bent half over with his head inside the cab window. He paid the fare along with a twenty dollar tip. He stood in front of the high rise office building on Decatur. Across the street, The Hilton was almost as tall. The sun was up there somewhere but you couldn't tell that to Junior.

He walked into the lobby of the building that held the Morgan and Sims Company. The inside seemed more like the outside. High ceiling. He couldn't make out where it ended. Elevators to the far back. Shops and banks to the right and a restaurant to the left. Junior didn't know which way to turn. He felt about as out of place as a turnip in a tomato patch. Not only did he not know where to turn but he, along with other folks, noticed he may be a bit under-dressed. T-shirt, shorts and flip flops in a crowd of suits and fine Italian shoes.

"Sir. Excuse me, sir."

Junior turned around to face a tall fellow, at least six-five, wearing a white button-up shirt, tie, pressed blue slacks, more like shined boots than dress shoes and a name tag that said 'James'.

"Can't help but notice that you look a bit lost. Might I help you? Maybe direct you?"

"Well, yes sir. I guess you could. I was looking for Morgan and Sims Company."

"Okay, that's by appointment only. If you would step with me over to the desk, we will give them a call.'"

From a few feet behind them:

"Jamie, Jamie! I got this. He is a friend."

"Sure thing, Miss Wells."

"Junior, what in the world are you doing here??"

She smiled again…. with the cold eyes.

5

John Wayne got dressed. Jeans, Hawaiian short-sleeved shirt with flowers and tennis shoes. An act of conforming that he performed usually once a month. He had even shaved and pulled his hair back into a ponytail.
He fed Butch and made sure his water dish was full and then set out on a trek up to the diner.

Out the front door, which he left wide open for Butch; in fact, he left the front door open most of the time until it got too cold. He took a step down from the little porch. Butch sat up, stretched, yawned and gave a whimper. JW turned and sat on the edge of the porch next to Butch.
"I guess we haven't had a chat for awhile. I do have a few things on my mind I would like to unload."

Butch sat up, cocking his head with a closed mouth as though ready to do some serious listening.

"Butch, I got to tell you. Sometimes my belief in God weakens somewhat. I shake it off and think it has got to take too much wasted effort to believe all of this ~ everything ~ came from nothing... than it is to believe there is a God that started it all. I mean, really Butch, did you come from nothing?"

Butch sat up straight, his tongue fell out the side of his mouth and he whimpered.

"Well, there could be some doubt about you. I mean, none of us are sure where *you* came from."

Butch stood on all fours and gave out a bark. JW looked into Butch's large brown eyes and knew.

"Nope, I'm sure you are God's work."

He gave Butch a pet on the head.

"I'm headed to the diner for a burger. I'll bring you one back."

Butch laid back down, curled up and was snoring before JW got five steps away.

The door opened to the diner mid-morning and Sylvia looked up from pouring coffee for Bob, the mailman, the only customer. "For goodness sake, look what the cat drug in! JW, I'll be right with you. Take a seat." He walked to the very last booth and sat with his back against the wall which had a good view of the front door.

This time Sylvia, in full character, came to JW's booth with three buttons of her uniform undone. She bent over the table resting on it with her elbows. JW had trouble breaking away from the view.
"So, what can I get for ya, hon?"
"Hamburger, everything but ketchup, fries, sweet tea."
"Cheese?"
"That would be a *cheese*burger, dear."
"Got ya."

Sylvia quickly returned with JW's tea.
"Your burger will be right out."
"While you're at it, will you put in an order
for another burger to go? Hold everything
but the meat."
"For Butch."
"Yep."
"I'll get it ready."
She smiled and walked away.

JW sat and watched her walk away. The
big bow on the back of her apron swung
from side to side. He watched the door and
windows that lined up with the booths
down the isle. Outside turned from a bright
sunshiny day to dark clouds and sheets of
rain in 3 seconds flat. Alabama weather
gonna fool you every time.

Sylvia came back with his burger and fries
and a stuffed to-go bag.
"You will find an extra patty in there. It's
on me. You be sure and tell Butch."
There was a fourth button undone on her

uniform and JW forgot everything else.
She leaned over to leave his ticket on the
table and said, "I get off at three."
JW cleared his throat and took a sip of tea.
"I think I'll hang around till three. Maybe
you can come over and tell Butch
yourself."
Sylvia winked and walked back to talk to
Bob.

The afternoon drifted on. The rain stopped
and the sun came back. Three o'clock
came and the walk to JW's shack was
pleasant.   Sylvia took a shower and JW
gave Butch his burgers, poured wine and
thought about Junior.

6

Now the hustle bustle all around Junior was almost overwhelming. People coming and going. All talking at the same time. It all ran together. Glenda waved her hand in front of Junior's face.

"Earth to Junior!"

He came around and smiled.

"My gosh, how do you put up with all this everyday??"

"What…." she asked.

"Okay. That explains it."

She looked confused and looked around seeing nothing unusual.

"Say Junior, you hungry?"

"I'm always hungry. I guess since it's so late I should walk across the street and get a room."

"It's the Hilton, Junior, it's going to be pricey."

"Price doesn't matter as long as when I shut
the door to my room, I can't hear all of
this."
She laughed. "I'm sure it will be quiet. So
do you like steak?"
"Love steak."
"You ever have a Ruth's Chris steak?"
"Don't even know what that is."
"Go check in, Junior, then meet me right
over there."
She pointed to the other side of the lobby.
"At the restaurant with the red sign. I'll get
us a table and then wait out front."
Junior nodded and walked to the revolving
doors.
She called back to him. "Maybe you should
pick up a pair of long pants in the Hilton
shop while you're at it."
He gave her a thumbs up.

Junior checked in to the Hilton. When the
lady at the counter noticed there was no
limit on the Master Card Junior used from
the Daleville Bank, where ever that was,

she became a little animated.
"Mr. Barns. if there is anything you need just ring me, please. Will you be staying just the one night?"
Junior paused with *'a thank you ma'am'* and a *'probably, but not sure'*.
"Just let me know, Mr. Barns."
Junior asked which way to the shop. The lady told him with a huge smile:
"Just down the hall to your left. Tell them to charge it to your room. Pick out what ever you like."

Junior enjoyed his shopping experience. He picked out some loose fitting pants with lots of wiggle room, a belt, a pullover shirt with a little alligator on the pocket. A bottle of cologne by Chanel. Two magazines and a western paperback. He kept his Crocs and left his old clothes in the try-on stall. He asked the cashier if she would have the cologne and books delivered to his room.

Back across the street he met Glenda at the door of the restaurant.

First came the bread, butter and wine. The wine, a foreign name with an old date, probably cheap but tasted good.
A few minutes passed before the waiter returned to their table asking them if they'd like to order. Junior explained that he would like a T-bone grilled to a temperature where he could hear the cow moo when he bit into it. The waiter laughed and walked swiftly to the kitchen to get their salads.

Junior could feel he was being taken for a ride. He took a sip of his wine, wishing he had ordered a beer.
"I know you really want to talk me into selling my land, but it's not going to happen. I think it might be best if we have this meal, call it an evening and I'll make my way back home tomorrow. I have no idea what I was thinking coming up here."

She stood, slammed her napkin down on
the table and walked out the door.

Junior finished his steak, potato and salad.
Maybe the best he ever had. Finished the
bread off. He finished the wine too and
ordered another bottle. Then there was
coffee and dessert. The waiter brought the
check and Junior asked if he was kidding.
The waiter smiled.
"Well, the young lady did order expensive
wine."
He stood there starting to doubt if Junior
could pay for the meal. Finally, Junior
pulled out his credit card and when the
waiter returned, Junior left a three hundred
dollar tip and slipped out the door.

Somewhere in the late night before sunrise,
Junior was awoken by a rap on the door. It
took him several seconds before he was
able to get out of bed, grab a towel from the
bath and open the door. There stood
Glenda, nude except for high heels.

Holding an ice bucket with a bottle of Dom
and a coat draped over her left arm, she
asked:
"You have glasses?"

7

The ringing of the phone, flashing of the
red message light and pounding at the door
aroused Junior enough to open one eye.
Laying across the bed sideways with the
towel still wrapped around him, he began to
sit up. More pounding at the door and
Junior called out, "Coming, coming!!" But
it only came out as a whisper. He looked
over at the clock on the bedside table. Four
thirty. *What the hell at four thirty in the
morning is going on?? Must be a fire,*
Junior thought and then he noticed light
coming in through the curtains. The rap at
the door came again. Junior managed to
get up and stumble to the door.

"I'm so sorry, sir. My name is Perkins.
I'm from the front desk and we just wanted
to check on you. You didn't answer your
phone and we needed to confirm your stay

for another evening and of course make sure you were okay."

Junior just stood there thinking, *what a perfect name for someone from the front desk.*

"Are you okay, sir???"

Junior wiped his face and opened both eyes.

"Yes, yes. I'm okay. Maybe a little too much to drink. Put me down for another night, would you, Perkins?"

"Yes sir, my pleasure." And he walked away.

Junior closed the door, turned facing the room and flipped the lights on. Over to the right on the desk in front of the mirror sat the bottle of Dom in the ice bucket. Uncorked with maybe a quarter of the champagne missing. A full glass sitting on the desk. A glass laying on the floor with a wet spot. No Glenda in sight. A file folder sat next to the bucket. Junior picked it up,

opened it.
A promise to sell contract.
Five pages with Junior's signature and
notarized at the end. A contract to sell his
land at fair market price. An option to turn
down three bids but to accept the highest.

Junior threw the file across the room. He
walked to the bathroom and washed his
face.
Back out in the bedroom, he stopped cold.
His pants and shirt were gone.
….and so was his wallet.

8

JW got dressed. Something he had never
done twice in one month. Unprecedented,
as the news would say. He gave Butch
food and water then set out for the dinner.

Sylvia, Bob, the postman, JW and Wilbur
from Wilbur's Tire and Auto all sat at the
counter. They all had coffee. Sylvia spoke
first.
"So none of you guys have heard from
Junior?"
They looked at each other and Wilbur
spoke.
"No, ma'am and it just ain't like Junior to
go out of town much less stay overnight."
JW looked over at Sylvia.
"Say you got any of that apple pie?"
She got up and went to the kitchen. JW
turned to Wilber.
"You know I can't remember in the

seven years I've been here that he went anywhere overnight."
Bob the postman set his cup down.
"I remember, maybe 10 years ago, he rode over to New Brockton to visit that musician friend of his. You know the one that married Miss New Brockton."
Both Sylvia and Wilbur remembered Miss New Brockton. Wilbur grinned.
"Yes sir, a real looker."
"Anyway, he made it over there but they all had a few too many beers and Junior called Chief Higgins over at the police station and told him he wouldn't be home."
JW said, "By the way, where is Higgins?"
Wilbur said, "He had the bug again and is laid up at home. I talked to him earlier and he ain't heard from Junior."
Sylvia slapped the counter.
"Somebody needs to go check on Junior, damn it!"
JW looked up from his coffee
"Y'all all know I don't fly and I can't drive. But I'll pay for whoever goes."

Bob stood and flipped his usual three
dollars on the counter.
"I got the mail. I can't go out of town."
Sylvia said, "Wilbur, you're gonna have to
do it."
"Miss Sylvia, I never been on a plane and
I'm not so sure I would fare well in the big
city."
The phone next to the cash register rang.
Sylvia stretched across the counter and
grabbed the handset. She sat back on her
stool.
"It's Junior, y'all!"
She spoke little into the phone and just
listened. Then slowly hung up.
"He says he needs for the bank to get him a
couple thousand dollars and a new credit
card to him as fast as possible. He's at the
Hilton on Decatur. He says he's okay."
Bob paused at the door.
"I'll see to it he has it tomorrow."
Everyone turned back to their coffee and
pie. They talked about Fort Rucker and
how it helped their little town. Sylvia
refilled their cups.

9

Decatur Avenue, 65th floor, corner office. Donald Webb closed the door behind Glenda. Eight o'clock in the evening and darkness now covered Atlanta. The view, almost breathtaking facing the city. The lights glowed and twinkled as far as the eye could see. The high rises and low rise shopping centers all lit up made the city look like a wonderland at night.

Webb poured splashes of Johnny Walker Blue into two short Waterford crystal glasses. He dropped a perfectly square ice cube in each. Glenda stood looking out the ceiling-to-floor windows and turned as Webb handed her a glass. He stood beside her as they both took their first sips.
"I assume you have good news."
She looked at him with the warm smile and cold eyes and then walked over to the chair

where she had left her bag. She pulled out
two files and placed them on his desk.
"The file in the blue folder is a contract to
leave Mr. Barns alone but to be first in line
if he ever wants to sell. The file in the
green folder is a promise to sell."
Webb took a sip from his drink and sat
down behind his desk. He picked up the
files and began to look through them.
"If you notice, the last page of both
contracts reads the same. I have now
swapped the last page of each contract.
The strong part of this little charade is that
there are two witnesses and a notary. I'll
spare you the details."

Webb opened his desk drawer and pulled
out a pack of Winston Lights. He took a
Ronson lighter from his pocket and lit the
cigarette. He blew out the smoke.
"You are a true artist." He smiled.
"You should get away for a few days.
Relax... let me handle the rest of this.
Maybe Florida. Suntan oil, margaritas. I'll

pick up the tab."
She winked and walked out of his office.

Three doors down from Schooners Beach
Bar in Panama City Beach in a two
bedroom townhouse, Glenda laid on a
towel in the sugar white sand. Once blond
hair, now jet black. Bright red lips and
nails, working on a dark tan. *A Double
Shot of my Baby's Love* blew from the
Schooners speakers. The waves lapped on
the shore. Way out in the Gulf, a dark
cloud formed and you could see a wall of
rain falling. A shadow blocked out the sun.

Glenda pulled her sunglasses down. It took
a few seconds before she could focus on the
figure standing beside her. Junior stood
there in his new long pants with another
pullover shirt with a little alligator on the
pocket. He wore his Crocs and was
holding two margaritas in plastic cups from
Schooners.
"Miss me?"

She never dropped her composure for a
second. She reached around, tied her bikini
top and sat up.
"Why Junior, I was just thinking about
you."
"Glenda, I just dropped by to tell you I
forgive you completely. Man, you got me.
I do have some lawyers over in Dale
County working on that bogus document
you duped me into signing. And as bad as
I hate to tell you, you're going to have to
move and complete your vacation
someplace else. You see, I own this town
house and the next four in the row. I have
to do some emergency repairs and of
course, you will get a full refund."

She stood and took one of the drinks from
Junior.
"You don't think I really believe you own
these four houses on the beach, do you?"
Junior smiled.
"How long... just how long have you
owned this beachfront property??"

She sipped her drink and stared at him with an icy glare.

The dark cloud that was brewing out in the Gulf was moving onto shore and large rain drops were beginning to pound the sand. Junior stood as though he was lost in thought for a few seconds.
"I don't have a watch but I'd say about two hours by now."
"I don't believe you."
"Yep. Miss Bevel who lives two doors down owned all four and rented three of them out. I asked her how much. She told me. I wired the money to her bank and she signed over the deeds with the stipulation that she could continue to live where she is until she dies, rent free, of course. I agreed. It's a done deal."

The cloud opened up and the rains came down. Junior made his way back to Schooners while Glenda stood there in the rain in utter shock.

10

Junior made it to the back door of
Schooners before getting too wet. He
knocked the sand off his Crocs and walked
up the steps around to the bar. He sat on a
stool on the far side so he had the best view
of the Gulf. He ordered smoked tuna dip
and another margarita from a cute little red-
headed waitress with a rag hanging from
the back pocket of her cut-off jeans. She
had a killer smile and was completely
focused on her job. Junior liked that and
asked for extra jalapeños. She had them
out before the dip arrived. Junior decided
his tip would make her year.

The rain outside came down with a
vengeance but only lasted for twenty
minutes. It came to an abrupt stop as
Junior was ordering a blackened grouper
sandwich. The sandwich was excellent.

Junior ordered another margarita from the cute redhead and relaxed while watching for Glenda.

Not long after the rain stopped, she came out of the back door of the townhouse wearing a conservative cover-up over her small swimsuit. Down the steps, she headed west to the third townhouse in the row. Up the steps, onto the deck, she knocked on the screen door. It was more of a flutter than a knock because the door did not completely shut. The first thing that hit Glenda was the reek of well-used cat litter. Then the overwhelming scent of tobacco smoke. The sound of rattling coughs and gagging. A wheezing voice said,
"Yes, yes. Come in." between coughs.

Glenda opened the door and weaved her way through the kitchen around litter boxes and cats. Passing from the kitchen into the front family room, Miss Bevel sat in a huge

Lazy Boy recliner. The only furniture in
the room other than a chairside table was a
boombox on the floor blaring out talk radio.
On the table sat a large ashtray full of
cigarette butts and a lit cigar burning away.
Three empty Busch beer bottles and a glass
filled with false teeth. Miss Bevel held a
copy of Woman's Day and through the
hacks and wheezing coughs asked,
"Well now, Missy. How can I help YOU?"

Glenda was barefoot. She stood on tip toes
trying to reach above the cloud of smoke to
take a breath. She just made it and sucked
in a lungful of cat poop smell. She gagged
and coughed. Miss Bevel gagged and
coughed. Glenda ran out of the room
through the kitchen, out onto the back deck
and drew in all the fresh air she could hold.
Hands on knees, she gasped for breath.

Junior watched from his seat at the bar. He
laughed and call to the redhead for his

ticket. She punched the buttons on the
register and handed him an itemized list of
his bill. He handed her his Master Card.
She brought back his final check with room
for a tip and his signature. She asked if
everything was good and he told her *just
right.*
Junior left enough tip to pay her rent for
several months.   He walked away and was
out the front entrance headed to his pick-up
before she ever looked at the ticket.

Glenda walked out onto the sand with her
hands on her hips, still gasping for air. She
turned with her back to the Gulf looking at
the townhouse wondering what had just
happened.

11

JW and Butch sat on the porch of his shack. Sometime JW thought about God as Junior does. Today he thought war was such a waste of God's children. Greed and bickering was such a waste of God's time. Love, smiles, laughter are a blessing from God. Maybe the best is a sense of humor.

JW could see Sylvia as she came from the highway to the lane and down the hill around to this side of the lake. She carried a sack. JW patted Butch on the head.
"I think there is a treat in your future, old boy."
Sylvia sat the sack down on the pier. She let her uniform drop off, stepped out of it and slid into the water. JW got up and walked out onto the pier and joined her.

The evening was filled with laughter, steaks
on the grill, wine along with a couple of
hamburgers for Butch. As Sylvia fell
asleep in JW's bed, he sat on the porch with
his last glass of wine and in a cloud of
concern for Junior. He wasn't sure where it
was coming from but he couldn't shake it.

12

Glenda stomped from the beach into the townhouse where she had been asked to leave. She picked up the phone by the bed and made the call to Atlanta as she packed her suitcase. She filled it with mostly swimsuits, a few pairs of shorts, a sundress along with make-up and such.

The phone rang twice at Morgan and Sims. She was placed on hold but it only took a few seconds before Donald Webb answered. She rattled away at what she had been through and what she had learned from Junior.
"I'll handle this now but best you head on back to Atlanta." And he hung up.

Webb made a call to Northern Bay County Florida then sat back, lit a Winston Light and poured a shot of Johnny Walker.

Junior walked to the back of Schooners'
parking lot across the street from the club.
Windows were down and the key left in
the ignition of the old '69 bucket of rust but
it was still there. He climbed in, fired it up
and tuned the radio to The Great 108 where
they proudly announced they were Number
2 in the Bay County rankings because all
the rest of the stations in the county were
Number 1.
Junior pulled the gear shift down into first,
spun some dirt across the lot and headed
down Thomas Drive, over to Back Beach
Road, then up Highway 79. Two hours to
Daleville would be an easy ride.

Across the West Bay Bridge and around the
long curve, he nearly ran into the back of a
barely moving old Massey Ferguson.
Junior had to break hard while listening to
Linda Ronstadt singing *You're No Good*.
A fairly new Dodge van pulled up behind
him and all vehicles came to a stop. Junior

reached behind him to grab the 12 gauge
double barrel... only it wasn't there. He
had taken it into the cabin for cleaning and
never put it back in the truck. He was now
having a feeling that this was a bad
mistake.

Two big fellows stepped out of the van. A
even bigger fellow climbed down from the
tractor. Junior stepped out of his truck.
Mistake Number Two. One of the fellows
from the van standing right in front of
Junior said,
"How 'bout a little ride, Junior!"
Junior noticed the other guy from the van
was holding a baseball bat. That was the
last thing he remembered...

Carl "Skinny" Brown pulled his F-150 over
to the side of the road where he saw
Junior's truck resting in a ditch. Skinny
stepped out of his truck - all 325 pounds of
him. He wore overalls, no shirt, sported a

straw hat and size 16 boots. Walking down
to the truck in the ditch is when he noticed
through a clearing, out in a freshly plowed
field, a naked man laying still. As Skinny
approached the fellow, he could see the
man had been beat to a pulp and the poor
guy had a long rope tied to his testicles. A
trail clearly showed where he had been
dragged around the field.

Skinny climbed back in his truck, made a
U-turn on Highway 79 and floored it back
to the Sip and Save in West Bay. He called
911.

The sun was within minutes of setting over
West Bay. You could see red lights flashing
for miles on Highway 79. The sheriff, high
way patrol and ambulance were all on the
scene. Skinny gave his full deposition to
the sheriff ending with
"And the worst part is that poor bastard is
still alive after being drug by his balls all
over that field."

Skinny walked away headed back to his truck, then turned back to the sheriff.
"You know them old boys need to be messed up for doing this."
Sheriff John Lee Rainey tipped his hat in agreement.

Skinny watched as the ambulance pulled away with lights flashing and siren blaring. He wished the poor fellow well, climbed back in his truck and headed north to Slocomb.

Junior lay perfectly still in the back of the ambulance. The pain was overbearing.
The EMT told him to hang on.
Junior said "okayyy" then the world went black.

13

Donald Webb poured another shot of Scotch, lit another Winston Light and made another phone call.

After four rings: "Rice here."

"Colonel Rice, I need to know how much longer I have on the Dale County property."

"Not long, Webb. I'm going to have to go public next week. But no one will know how much the government is willing to pay for that land in Daleville. That knowledge is only yours, and I expect a reward."

"Good. A week is all I need. You will get our agreement."

"Webb, we never talked. Understand?"

"I do."

The line went dead. Webb put out his cigarette, downed the last of the Scotch and left his office.

14

Heading up Highway79 just past Holmes Creek, Skinny was thinking deeply about the poor fellow he had found in the field. He hoped he would be okay and wouldn't have to wear pants with three legs the rest of his life.

He looked in the rear view mirror of his F-150 and saw a white Dodge van approaching fast. Skinny took his foot off the gas in hopes of slowing the van. The van actually sped up, swerving to pass Skinny, running a Chevy Nova off the road. As the van passed Skinny, the passenger waved a baseball bat out the window. Skinny thought for a second that enough bad had happen on his normally peaceful trip home. He mashed the gas, the truck gave a buck of protest but then caught and sailed up 79. Skinny was closing in on the van when a strange thing happen. The right rear tire on the van blew. The Dodge swerved right, then left, then all the way around, almost tipping over. It slid into a ditch just missing the driveway of an old farmhouse.

Mr. Kyle Stone got up from his rocking chair on the porch where he was watching the whole event. He called for his wife Emma and continued to watch as an F-150 pulled up by the van. Kyle and Emma stood on their porch and watched as Skinny stepped down from his truck. The springs on the F-150 gave out a sigh. Skinny walked up to the van and could smell the beer when he got close. The two fellows stumbled from the van, the one on the passenger side still holding the baseball bat. Skinny shouted out as he surveyed the situation.
"You boys okay?!"

Standing in front of Skinny, the driver
looked at the van and then at Skinny.
"We're good, but we are going to need to
borrow your truck, fat man."
"I don't think so, but maybe I could give
you boys a lift."
"Fat man, you don't want us to give you
what we gave the fellow down by West
Bay."

The one with the bat stood rocking back
and forth. He raised the bat. It only took
200 of Skinny's 325 pounds to snatch the
bat away and crack the man's skull.
"Okay, fat man, you just......."
Before he could finish his thought, Skinny
flipped the bat over and swung. The nub of
the bat tore the fellow's nose completely
off. Skinny looked up at the folks on the
porch and hollered,
"Y'all might want to call 911!"
Emma ran inside to the phone.

The old boy with the missing nose lay on

the ground wailing. The other one was
barely breathing.
Skinny thought to himself, 'I think you
boys are messed up enough.'

He turned and climbed back into his truck
and headed on to Slocomb.

15

Monday morning, two days after Junior was beaten up and dragged around the field, he opened his eyes in a double room in Bay Medical. The fellow in the bed next to him had tubes running out of him. He was moaning and groaning and calling out for someone named Nina. Junior closed his eyes again thinking he would go back to sleep or go back to where ever he was... when a voice interrupted all of that.
"Mr. Barns, I need you to take these pills and I need to get your temperature."
"Who are you???"
"My name is Amy. I just started Saturday when they brought you in. I'm looking after you and Mr. Johnson over there and Miss Ellis in the room across the hall. Mr. Johnson's wife should be here soon and he will quiet down."
"His wife, Nina??"

"No sir. His wife, Joan. I'm not sure who
Nina is."
Junior convinced himself that Amy was an
angel. She sure looked like one anyway.

For the next few days, every time Junior
opened his eyes she was there. After
Amy pulled the thermometer from Junior's
mouth and confirmed it was normal, Junior
asked:
"I got to tell you. I feel like death warmed
over. How bad is it?"
"Mr. Junior, I feel like you're a lucky man
after hearing what you went through. Your
doctors should tell you but, you do have a
broken rib, a cracked jaw and more bruises
than the law should allow. The swelling
between your legs should eventually go
down. If not, you might want to consider a
career in porn. It's quite impressive."
Junior tried to laugh but it hurt way too
bad. He had to leave it with a smile.

Later that afternoon, Amy pushed Junior to

down some strawberry Jello. He tried his
best. The first bite went down but the
second, no way. He spat it out in the bed
pan.

Doctor Juan Cortez entered the room with
his entourage of three nurses and two
interns.
"Mr. Junior, how are you today?"
That's where he stopped. He noticed the
red in the bed pan. He ordered everyone
out of the room. He called the nurses'
station to put Junior in quarantine right
away. Full shut down. No one could enter
without masks and hazmat suits. Alarms
and flashing lights went off. Junior wanted
to laugh but it hurt too much.

Sheriff Rainey called the number he found
in Junior's wallet. It was the diner's
telephone. Sylvia answered. The sheriff
told her what had happened. She told the
sheriff she would be there in a few hours.

16

The phone rang four times at the diner. The rule was that Earl The Cook would answer after four rings. It meant Sylvia was busy waiting on customers. Earl had been the cook at the Daleville Diner for over ten years now. His claim to fame was making the perfect soft scrambled eggs and he did. Folks would drive from Enterprise to have breakfast.
Sylvia was waiting on two Black Hawk pilots and doing her usual flirt when Earl called out,
"Phone, Sylvia! It's about Junior."
She stopped flirting mid-sentence and ran for the phone.

When Sylvia hung up, she called Daleville Tire and Auto. Wilbur answered. Before he could complete his phone opening speech, Sylvia interrupted.

"Junior is in bad shape at the hospital in
Panama City. We need to go right now and
your the only one that I know that has a
vehicle in good enough shape to make the
trip."
"You mean my tow truck??"
"It will have to do. It'll hold three of us,
won't it?"
"Three *should* be able to squeeze in the
front seat. Never tried it."
"Drop what you're doing. Pick me up at
the diner. We'll swing by and pick up JW
on the way."
Before Wilbur could explain he had a
business to run, Sylvia had hung up.
"Damn woman," Wilbur cussed as he threw
his wrench down and locked the doors on
The Tire and Auto.

Wilbur and Sylvia pulled around the lane in
front of the lake and Junior's cabin. JW
saw them from the porch of his shack.
Wilbur yelled out as they approached.

"Dad gum, JW! Don't you ever wear
anything??"
"Not if I can help it."
Sylvia rolled her eyes.
"Get dressed, JW. Junior needs us down in
Panama City."
JW did not have to be told twice. He
stepped inside the shack and pulled on
shorts, t-shirt and slipped into flip flops.
He grabbed his wallet and the three of them
ran to the truck.

Flying down 79, Wilbur noticed a white
Dodge van in a ditch beside the road out in
front of a farm house. He thought *there's
an easy fifty bucks'* but he drove on by
headed south.

By mid-afternoon, the tow truck pulled into
the side parking lot at Bay Medical. Wilbur
noticed the temperature gauge had run over
into the hot zone.
"Confound, if I've blown up my truck, I'm
gonna be pissed."

JW leaned over.

"Calm down. If your truck is messed up, I'll buy you a new one."

The three of them jumped out and ran to the emergency entrance on the side of the hospital.   Down the long hall to the front entrance, they ran into a fellow in a white doctor's smock ranting and raving in Spanish. He was toting a box full of personal items and being escorted by a security guard. The guard tapped the fellow on the shoulder.

"By the way, Dr. Cortez, I'll be needing your badge."

The fellow in the white coat pulled the badge from around his neck and threw it on the floor.

Sylvia, JW and Wilbur rushed on passed to the front desk and found out what room Junior was in.

By the time the three of them made it up to Junior's room he was out of quarantine and back in his room next to Mr. Johnson…. moaning and groaning and calling for Nina.

17

Glenda Wells opened the door to Donald
Webb's office without knocking.
Bypassing his secretary, she slipped in and
closed the door behind her. Webb hated
this but held his words. She walked over to
his desk, sat on the corner and crossed her
legs. High heels, no stockings. Webb had
to pause his train of thought.
She gave a slight smile.
"So, should I pack for Jamaica yet?"
Webb dropped his displeasure of her
entering his office unannounced and smiled
back.
"Soon, dear. Our team of lawyers are
backing those yahoos down in Alabama.
This land deal will go through soon and I'll
have more money than the two of us can
count. Using the company's weight, they
will never even know about the deal and we
will be long out of here."

He turned the dial on the safe that was built
into the right side of his desk.   It swung
open and he pulled out an envelope,
handing it to Glenda. It was a fake
passport, driver's license and social
security card.
He walked over to his office door and
locked it, then poured two rounds of
Johnny Walker.

18

Junior tried his best not to move. It seemed he hurt in less places like that. Mr. Johnson in the next bed was quiet for the first time. Junior's eyes almost fell shut.

Sylvia was the first one in the door. She cried out:
"Junior! Ohhh baby! What in the world has happened to you?!"
She ran around the bed and hugged on Junior. *He* wanted to cry out but somehow didn't.
Mr. Johnson cried out, "Nina!"

JW and Wilbur stood at the door. Wilbur's mouth fell open. Sylvia stood back up and lifted the sheet to see what all was wrong with Junior. She screamed. JW and Wilbur ran around the bed to look. JW couldn't turn away.

"Dude, what in the hell took place here?!
This is pretty damn impressive!"
Wilbur was speechless. He could only
stand there with his mouth hanging open.
Sylvia lowered the sheet.
"Oh Junior honey, what can I do?"

Junior almost replied but the door opened
and it was Amy toting a big vase of
flowers. She sat them on Junior's bedside
table.
"Junior, you want me to read you the
card?"
Junior squeezed out, "Please."
"It's from Mrs, Bevel, the cat lady. She
says prayers for your fast recovery and if
you need anything at all to let her know."
Amy put the card back on its little holder in
the vase.
"How sweet."
Junior nodded and smiled. Amy looked
over at Sylvia.
"So I guess you are Junior's friends from
Daleville?"

Sylvia nodded in acknowledgement.
"We came as soon as we heard. Is anything broken, I mean, is he going to be alright?"
"Nothing broken, just a lot of bruising and swelling. He's lucky but he is going to hurt for a while, I'm afraid. Listen, I'm going to leave you guys alone but don't stay too long. He needs his rest."
JW thanked her as she left the room.

Junior looked over at JW.
"If you can find my truck, in the glove box are the keys and deeds to the townhouses I bought over on the beach. Y'all can stay in them."
"You bought townhouses??"
"It's a long story."
Wilbur said, "I can't stay. I got a business to run."
"Yes and I got a job that needs me," Sylvia said.
JW announced that he could stay.
"Wilbur, will you be able to check on Butch?"

"No problem. I may even take him to work
with me."

The three left discussing the details and
telling Junior to rest. Junior closed his eyes
and could feel sleep on the way.

Dr. William Bliss pushed open the door and
came into the room whistling. Dressed in
jeans, flannel shirt with the sleeves rolled
up, tennis shoes. No white smock, no
stethoscope, only a hospital name tag. He
walked around to Junior's bedside.
"Mr. Barns."
Juniors eyes flew open after coming so
close to sleep. The doctor slapped two
fingers on Junior's neck. After a few
seconds, he turned and grabbed a chair
from across the room. Mr. Johnson called
out for Nina. Dr. Bliss turned the chair
around backward and straddled it. Junior
asked, "How am I doing, Doc?"
"You tell me first, Mr. Barns."
"I feel like shit, Doc."

"That's a fair description of the way you look too, but in a few days the cuts and bruises will start to fade and heal. The swelling should go down in a week or so."
"What if it don't, Doc?"
Dr. Bliss stood and put the chair back in place. He pull a notepad from his shirt pocket as he walked to the door.
"Then you will have a heck of a time wearing a Speedo this summer. Now you rest. It's most important."
He left the room and Junior closed his eyes again just as Amy entered the room with a cup of pills.

Wilbur dropped JW off at the sheriff's office and after signing papers and showing his ID, JW drove away in Junior's truck. JW stopped in at a Walmart and purchased jeans, a couple of t-shirts, one with Roll Tide across the front. He also picked up a Browning 12-gauge pump along with a box of shells. He put the Browning in the gun rack behind the seat and the shells in the glove box and headed to the beach.

He chose the townhouse next to Schooners.
After a shower and slipping into the jeans
and a t-shirt, he walked next door just in
time for the firing of Schooners' cannon at
sunset. As he sat at the deck bar, a cold
Bud and tuna dip started his evening.

19

JW sat on the stool at Schooners watching the sunset. He ordered another beer and began to admire his driving skills. It had been at least four years. Amazed that the fellow at the compound yard had not noticed his driver's license was three years out of date. He took another look at the menu and ordered a blackened grouper sandwich and a side salad with Thousand Island….thinking he could get used to the beach life.

Roy Fields, one of the attorneys working on the land case for Junior, studied his latest notes. He looked up from the papers in front of him around the table at his team of lawyers, and then down at the end of the table at Judge Ledgen. Seven o'clock in Ozark, Alabama downtown at Fields office on Andrews Avenue.

"Fellows, it looks like the guys in Atlanta
have got us. I don't see any way out of this
contract."
Judge Ledgen stood.
"And I can't make a ruling unless we have
something to stand on. Someone needs to
tell Junior!"
Everyone got up from their chairs, tired
from being there for most of the day.
"I'll get word to him," Roy said.

Darkness fell on the beach. The sound of
the waves relaxed JW even more than he
normally was. Two guys inside on the
stage with guitar, bass and a drum machine
struck up a tune. *Turn The Page* by Bob
Seger. This grabbed JW's attention and he
had to turn and listen.

A fax of 'no contest' rolled off Donald
Webb's fax just before midnight.

Junior finally fell asleep just as Mr.
Johnson cried out for Nina.

JW walked down the beach to the water's
edge just after midnight. He turned and
walked up to the townhouse and around to
the back deck. He pulled his clothes off
and stretched out on the lounge chair. He
fell asleep to the pounding of the waves.

20

Art Cotton slid the single sheet of paper across the conference table to Carl Riff - two of the more than one hundred lawyers in the firm who represented Morgan and Sims. Carl made a quick read of the document, then looked up at Art.
"We better go ahead and tell Webb and get it over with."

The two walked out of their building without putting on their coats. Up Decatur one block into the high rise that held Morgan and Sims. Up the elevator, they patiently waited while Donald Webb's secretary announced them. As they entered Webb was just pouring a splash of Scotch.
"Good to see you guys. I'm ready to move forward with this land deal. You guys care for a little Scotch?"
"No sir," Art said. "I'm afraid the news we have is not so good."

Webb sat down behind his desk and took a sip. "Oh??"
Carl took the lead.
"The title search came back today. Sorry it took longer that normal. The problem being it appears Junior Barns never owned that land he lives on."
"Go on." Webb took another sip.
"It seems the state of Alabama, way back, turned that land over to a Yellow Trace and Young Bird for the hardship they went through when the state was first being formed. Bottom line, it belongs to the Choctaw Indians."
Webb threw his glass against the far wall and it shattered into a hundred pieces.

Thirty minutes after the lawyers left, Webb had packed a few things into his briefcase. He had typed a letter to the company explaining that he would be gone for awhile. Then he buzzed Glenda Wells' office.
"Miss Wells if you could come to my office, please."

She came right away and Webb explained
to her that the land deal fell through and
that he was going to take some time off.
He stormed from his office. No one in the
company ever saw Donald Webb again.
Within two weeks, Glenda Wells moved
into Webb's office with the grand view
after completely ratting him out to the
company CEO. She sat behind his desk
and poured a splash of Scotch. She smiled
but with ice cold eyes.

The sun fell on JW's eyes and he sat up
from the lounge chair. He stood and
walked to the water's edge, then dove in for
a swim. As he was coming back out of the
water, he saw Miss Bevel standing on her
back deck. Cigarette in one hand, a beer in
the other. She coughed, wheezed and
waved at JW, smiling. Two red-headed
fellows jogged by him fussing at each other
over something. Never noticing JW.

JW walked up on the beach headed to the

townhouse when he spotted two Bay County sheriffs all dressed in green coming down the beach from Schooners. They met him as he was climbing the steps to the deck of the townhouse.

"Sir, we are going to have to ask you to put some clothes on."
JW looked down. "Oh, sorry 'bout that."
He reached down and picked up his t-shirt, slipping it on.
"Sorry 'bout that.   Just habit from back home."
"Maybe some pants too."
JW slipped on his jeans.
"Not sure where home is but it's against the law around there to be nude on the beach. Let's not let it happen again."
"Yes sir."
They walked on down the beach. JW turned and looked over his shoulder. Miss Bevel took a deep drag from her cigarette, coughed and waved at JW.

83

21

Wilbur pulled to a stop on Highway 79 at the four-way stop that intersected with Highway 52. Sylvia sat up in her seat becoming aware of where they were. "Slocomb tomatoes!! I want some Slocomb tomatoes. Wilbur, pull over to that stand!!"
She pointed to a produce stand just on the other side of 52. The sign above the open-air shed read *Skinny's Slocomb Tomatoes and Such*. Wilbur pulled over to the stand and parked out front.

Before them lay a world of fresh vegetables. Proudly displayed out front were baskets of beautiful tomatoes. All plump, the size of softballs. Stretched out on either side of the shed was a kaleidoscope of colors. Beans, peas, watermelon, squash, bell peppers, onions, cantaloupe and cucumbers.   Sylvia wanted

some of each but settled for a basket of tomatoes, a couple of large squash and a sweet Vidalia onion. A large fellow with a big grin and big boots met them at the counter where Sylvia had set her items.
"Will that be all for you good folks today?"
Sylvia smiled and paid for her goods. As Wilbur pulled back out on the highway, he said,
"You know, I like that fellow. Seems like a righteous kinda guy."
Sylvia nodded in agreement.

Butch slapped his tail against the floor of the porch on the shack so hard it made the boards rattle. Wilbur walked up to the porch and Butch sat up.
"You want to spend a few days with me, fella?"
Butch ran out and circled Wilbur's legs. He followed Wilbur to his truck and jumped in. The next few days, Butch spent learning the tire business.

With long pants and a t-shirt on, JW slipped
on flip flops, grabbed his wallet and walked
out the front door of the townhouse. He
walked one block over to Thomas Drive
and one block east to The Waffle Iron. He
sat behind the counter of a full house.
He ordered a waffle, two eggs over easy,
bacon, hash browns with onions, coffee and
orange juice. The waitress called out the
order to the lone cook with no written
instructions. Ten minutes later, his order
was served just as ordered. JW was well on
his way to a relocation to the beach.

Junior sat up in bed feeling almost human.
He looked forward to his breakfast for the
first time since he had been in the hospital.
The nurse came in with a tray. Eggs, grits,
coffee and orange juice.   He cleaned his
plate and finally felt he was well on his
way to recovery. He lifted the covers and
even though he felt almost normal, it
looked like the bull of a tribe was laying in
his bed. Most of the bruises were gone but

the swelling between his legs had not made
much progress. He closed his eyes in
hopes that it was all a dream but Mr.
Johnson again let out a call for Nina.

Junior was fading off to sleep thinking *who
was Nina???* just as Amy shook his
shoulder.
"I need to take your temperature, Mr.
Junior."

22

Junior watched as Amy left the room. She had checked his temperature, wished him good morning and looked at his swollen testicles maybe a little too long. Junior didn't mind. In fact, he had a bit of a smile on his face when he looked over at Mr. Johnson. For goodness sake, he was sitting up in bed reading a newspaper. He held the paper down a bit and peered over the top of his reading glasses at Junior.
"She's a cutie, isn't she..."
He flicked the paper back up around his face.
"Says here that President Ford made General Lee a citizen again."
Junior laid back.
"That's good. So who is Nina?"
He brought the paper down. "Nina?"
"Yeah, you keep calling out for Nina."

"Oh right. It's just a name I use to piss my wife off."

Junior smiled, closed his eyes. Mr. Johnson continued to read the paper until nine-thirty at what time he put the paper down, closed his eyes and cried out "Nina!" as his wife stepped into the room.

Junior thought about rolling over so she wouldn't see him laughing, then thought better of it. Rolling over on certain parts would not be good. He grinned and fell asleep just before Amy stood beside him with a cupful of pills.

JW walked back to the townhouse and climbed into Junior's truck. He took a deep breath knowing he had to make it all the way across town to the hospital without being pulled over. He cranked it, pulled the gearshift down into first, eased off the clutch and drove over to Thomas Drive. At the curve just past Montego Bay something pulled JW to go straight into Saint Andrews State Park. He paid his two dollars at the gate and drove on to the beach.

Standing on a dune overlooking the jetties
that lined the pass between the bay and
Gulf, he watched a large offshore ship
making its way to the big waters. It was a
hundred and fifty footer if it was an inch.
Painted boldly on the starboard side was
'The Just Right'. A fellow in an old t-shirt
with messy hair waved at JW from the
railing. JW waved back.

Now his focus took him to two fellows
standing on the jetties. Barefoot, pants
rolled up with reels and rods in hand. A
boy and his dad. Closer inspection showed
JW that it was him and his dad. He
remember the times well. His dad had an
old Pflueger Supreme reel. He claimed it
was the best ever built but every time he
cast it, enough line backlashed on the dang
thing to stop the prop on the *Just Right* that
had just passed. He would sit on the rocks

and untangle the coiled-up mess and never
say a curse word. JW never dared laugh.
The memory was priceless and with that,
JW walked back to the truck.

JW made it to the hospital and entered
Junior's room to find him sleeping. Mrs.
Johnson sat by her husband steaming as he
called out for Nina. JW made enough noise
dragging a chair around to the side of
Junior's bed to wake him up. Junior
opened one eye and before JW could say a
word -
"Doc says I can go home tomorrow
afternoon. I need a new t-shirt, new flip
flops, size 10 and a pair of triple x sweat
pants. I'll be needing some extra room.
We can stay at the townhouse for a while so
get some groceries."

Junior closed his eyes and turned his head.
JW dragged the chair back making a racket.
Mr. Johnson cried out, "Nina!" Mrs.
Johnson frowned. Junior smiled.

JW cautiously made his way onto 23rd
Street and pulled into the parking lot of
Walmart once again. He grabbed a buggy
and went on the hunt for a Panama City
Beach t-shirt, size 10 flip flops and a pair of
four x sweat pants. He figured the extra
room wouldn't hurt. Then he headed over
to the grocery side of the store and grabbed
a case of Miller, a pack of bologna, a pack
of cheese, three different kinds of potato
chips and a loaf of bread. Also, a can of
pork 'n beans and four Zero candy bars.

He checked out with a cashier named
Brittany who looked so good he tried to tip
her but she said it was against the rules.
When he handed her back the signed,
folded credit card receipt, there was a
hundred dollar bill tucked inside.

23

At one o'clock JW walked into Junior's room. He carried a Walmart bag with Junior's new duds. Junior sat on the side of the bed with a wheelchair already pulled up for him.

"It's about time," Junior said.

"Well, you said *afternoon*."

Junior slid off the bed and grabbed the bag from JW. He walked very gingerly to the bathroom. He returned all decked out and sat back down in the wheelchair.

"Let's get out of here."

JW swung the door open and pushed Junior out of the room. As they passed through the doorway, Mr. Johnson cried out "Nina!" Junior looked back at JW.

"For goodness sake, does he not know his wife is not there? What is wrong with him?"

JW pushed the chair onto the elevator

where the door was just opening. Out
stepped a blond, big hair, short dress, high-
heeled mules, tight sweater with absolutely
no bra.
"Could you gentlemen tell me which room
Mr. Johnson is in?"
Junior asked: "Ma'am, if you don't mind
me asking who you are."
"I don't mind at all. I'm Nina."
Almost speechless, Junior choked out
"Down the hall, first room to your right."

A few days at the townhouse on the beach
turned into a few weeks, then a month.
Three times a week Miss Bevel would
come coughing, wheezing and puffing
down the beach with a home-cooked meal
for supper. It was always wonderful and
both JW and Junior couldn't believe how
good it was. They always worried that she
wouldn't make it back home but somehow
she always did.
Sunsets on the deck with either beer or
wine became a routine.

Junior in the lounger with his 3x sweet
pants. JW in the rocker with a washcloth in
his lap. The music from Schooners made
the night pleasant. The sun sinking into the
Gulf. The young couples walking hand in
hand along the water's edge, the children
laughing and splashing in the waves. It all
made this time of day magical.

Junior took the last sip of his beer and sat
the bottle on the deck. He looked out over
the Gulf and then turned to JW.
"I'm ready to go back to Daleville."
JW was quick to respond.
"Me too."

24

Saturday morning Junior and JW packed up. It didn't take long. Two Walmart bags held all their stuff. They threw the bags in the truck and walked down the beach to Miss Bevel's house.

JW knocked on her back door but of course, there was no response. He opened the door and they went in. Around and over all the cat litter boxes, bowls of food and water. They made it to the livingroom despite the smell. Miss Bevel sat in her chair, this time with headphones on. The TV flashed with a local channel. She was smoking a cigarette with an ashtray beside her on the little table... slam full, running over with butts and ashes. Three empty beer bottles stood on the table and one half full in her hand. Her foot kept time to the music filling her head through the headphones. They stood there and waited

for her to pull the headphones off. She
smiled with her brown teeth but it was a
genuine smile. Junior spoke.
"Miss Bevel, we just wanted to thank you
for all the meals."
He handed her a slip of paper with his
phone number.
"You ever need anything, you call me. Do
you understand?"
The smile stayed on her face with maybe a
tear slipping out from her eyes.

JW, feeling a bit awkward, picked up the
ashtray and took it into the kitchen to
empty it. The garbage was overflowing
with ashes, beer cans and empty cat food
bags. He picked up the garbage, a lot
spilling over onto the floor, to take outside
to her City can. It was overflowing too.
He sat the can down and walked back into
the house.

Miss Bevel looked up at Junior.
"You boys be careful going home."

She coughed and wheezed.
"Your purchase of the townhouses saved
 me. Gave me a new life."

"I have retained Miss Jackson to rent and
look after the townhouses. You have any
problems at all with this one, you call her."
He handed her a card. He'd never seen her
smile nearly as big as she was now.
Junior and JW turned and left. They were
silent for the longest time. Both thinking of
what would happen to that woman.

At Highway 79, they both started talking at
once. Both wanting to say how glad they
were to be heading home. At the
intersection of Highway 52 over on the far
side of the road stood Skinny's Slocomb
Tomatoes. They saw a large man replacing
two baskets of tomatoes on the bench out
front. JW leaned over to Junior.
"Man, some Slocomb tomatoes sure would
be good."

"I know, JW, but I really need to get home. This ride is taking its toll on me."

Back in Daleville, they stopped at Daleville Tire and Auto. JW got out and a few minutes later, he and Butch jumped back into the truck. Butch went to licking Junior's face. A few minutes later, they pulled up to the cabin.

25

JW and Junior stepped out of the truck
along with Butch. Butch ran to the porch
of the cabin and flopped down asleep
before his next breath. Junior limped
toward the cabin.
"I love this place."
JW walked around the side of the cabin
toward the shack. He threw his t-shirt off
over his head to the right. He stepped out
of his flip flops and then out of his shorts.
"Me too, Junior! Me too!"

The following week was mostly uneventful.
Junior rested on the bed and switched to the
front porch when the spirit moved him. He
sipped a little wine and read a lot. He only
saw JW once at night when JW walked
down to the lake for a swim. Patch joined
him.

Saturday came around again and Junior
called out for JW.
"Let's ride around to the diner for lunch."

Junior drove and admitted to JW that he felt
a lot better. The swelling was mostly gone.

The reunion was good, familiar and smiling
faces. Bob, the mailman, was the first to
shake Junior's hand. Wilbur patted him on
the back. Sylvia hugged maybe a bit too
tight and whispered in his ear.
"I can't wait to see."
It took Junior about two seconds to not
think about sex.

As Junior headed for the back booth the
one guy sitting at the counter stood. Suit
pants, white shirt with rolled-up sleeves
and a loose tie. He stood by Junior and
asked,
"Are you Junior Barns?"
"Who wants to know."

"My name is Carl Riff and I'm here on behalf of Morgan and Sims. If I could just have a minute of your time."

Junior knew this couldn't be good.

"Sure. Have a seat."

Junior slid into the last seat facing the door. JW sat next to him and Riff parked in the seat on the other side of the table.

"I just want to put you aware that your land deal has taken a dramatic turn. It seems after extensive research you don't own the land you're living on. The Choctaw Indians do. The Choctaw tribe in charge of the land has issued a statement. Because of the time involved and how long you and your family have lived on the land, they listed a price for which they would take for the property. Even though you have first choice at purchase, the government has turned it down, and that's a whole other story. You have thirty days to commit to purchase or decline. After that the tribe will consider building a casino of which

Morgan and Sims will be heavily invested."
Riff handed Junior an envelope.
"Here is documentation of all that I have
said along with the amount wanted for the
land."
He got up and walked out of the diner.
Junior and JW sat with their mouths open.

Junior waited until he was home to open
the envelope. Late in the afternoon, out on
the front porch of the cabin with a glass of
wine, two for JW, he ripped open the
envelope. Four pages. The first three were
detailed proof of ownership. The last page
showed the amount to purchase.

"I have maybe half enough monry, even
with selling the townhouses in Florida.
And that would completely drain my
funds."
He handed the papers to JW.
"Well, hell. I got the other half, but it
would break me too."

The sun was setting on the far side of the
lake. Sylvia walked from the diner. Three
empty bottles of wine found Junior and JW
swimming in the lake. Butch lay on the
pier. Sylvia joined them. The three of
them laughed and splashed and howled at
the moon.

26

Monday morning late, Junior slowly rolled out of bed. Sylvia was long gone; she had to work. On the counter next to the coffee pot was a note from JW.
"I thought about it and decided it would be dumb to break myself on this property as much as I love it. You need me, I'll be in the townhouse on the beach. I'll gladly buy it from you. The bus leaves early and I got all my stuff in a Piggly Wiggly bag. Love ya, brother."

Junior got his coffee perking and walked out on the porch. Butch came from the side of the cabin and curled up by Junior's chair. Junior began to sit in his chair but stopped. Instead, he walked to the side of the cabin, cranked his truck and pulled it out front. He began with a vengeance loading what he could in the back of the truck.

Sipping his second cup of coffee, he looked
around thinking what he could not live with
out. Turned out not much. He unplugged
the coffee pot, emptied it and placed it in
the back of the truck. His pillows, porch
chair, clothes, cast iron pan and pot. Butch
jumped into the passenger side. Junior took
a long look at the lake and the cabin. He
hated leaving the old tractor but he drove
off past the lake and up to the highway.

Glenda Wells called her secretary in and
handed her an envelope.
"See to it that this envelope is overnighted
to the Choctaw land office in Montgomery,
Alabama."
She never got a return answer. She turned
her resignation in to the top floor crowd
and lost herself in the big city.

Down 84 nineteen miles, Junior could see
the four-way stop at Highway 52. He could
make out the vegetable stand on the right
side of the road. As he pulled into the

stand, he noticed a monster tent on the south side of 52. Like a circus tent but not as tall. He got out of the truck and open the door for Butch to jump down and do his business. Junior walked under the awning of the stand and was met by a large fellow. Overalls, big boots, jolly with rosy cheeks like Santa Claus. The big fellow looked at Junior hard for a second.

"You know who I am?"

Junior thought and said, "No, I don't guess I do. Hopefully the guy who will sell me some tomatoes."

"I'm the guy who saved you from the side of the road after who knows what all you had been through."

Junior stood for the longest time, speechless.

"Oh my gosh, I don't know what to say. I owe you my life!"

"Oh, don't mention it. It was kinda worth it when later I run up on those old boys. I got to mess them up pretty bad. Now that I know your alright, well, it's all good."

"I got to tell you…. I am totally
overwhelmed. How would I ever thank
you? I guess I'll start out by buying a
basket of tomatoes."
The big man smiled, nodded his head.
"An excellent choice."
Junior randomly pick up a basket and set it
on the counter.
"By the way, what's up with the big tent
across the road?"
"Jeremiah Stone is putting on a revival. A
preacher out of Dothan that folks can't
seem to get enough of. I'm gonna check
him out tonight myself."
Junior though for a second.
"Heck, I might hang around and check him
out too."
"You should, I think it would be worth it.
By the way, my name is Carl, Carl Brown.
Everyone around here calls me Skinny.
Listen, you are welcome to stay with me
and the misses."
"I'm Junior Barns. I do appreciate it but
me and Butch will be just fine in the truck.

I would like to park over here at your stand
if you don't mind."
"Oh heck no, make yourself at home."
Junior paid for his tomatoes and Skinny
closed up the stand for the day. As he
walked around to his truck, he called out to
Junior.
"See ya tonight about 7!"
Junior nodded.

27

Seven o'clock rolled around and Junior walked across the road to the tent. Highway 52 was normally not busy at all this time of night. Now folks were actually stopping at the four-way stop, some even having to wait on the next car. He left the truck door open and water for Butch.

The tent was almost full. Skinny, his wife and their daughter sat on the back row and had saved a chair for Junior. The chatter and hustle-bustle died down as the lights dimmed in the tent. No music, no introduction. A fellow stepped on the stage. Shaggy hair, blue jeans, t-shirt and tennis shoes. Forty-five minutes later Jeremiah Stone stepped off the stage. The lights in the tent came up and the very quiet crowd began to file out.

Short version, Jeremiah explained that a lot

of folks had no idea who or what God was.
They seemed to think that God Almighty,
the Creator of All, the everlasting power
over everything should think the way *they*
do. Why would a loving God allow pain
and suffering, allow cancer, deformed
children, war? Why would an all-knowing
God make so many design flaws? Thing is
there is no way any human could possibly
know what the God of everlasting power
thinks or reasons. We were made in the
same image, not the same intellect. He did
come to earth as a man. So he knows
exactly what we go through. He died to
save us from ourselves. We don't know
how that works. The important thing is we
know that it does. Our strive to be
important should end when we realize who
we are in God's eyes.

After the meeting, Junior was amazed at
how many folks greeted him. Not in long
conversation but, *'how you doin', good to
see ya, glad you could make it out.'*

This really made Junior feel at home.

Behind the tent were ten barrel grills in a row with folks cooking chicken. A quarter chicken, potato salad, green bean, a roll and sweet tea: a dollar. All went to the rent of the tent, none for Jeremiah. Rumor had it that Jeremiah even picked up the tab for the food. Two fellows who had to be twins served Junior two orders, one for Butch.

He said good night to Skinny and his family and as they began to pull out onto Highway 52, a red short-bed Chevy, tarp over the back, roared pass them, horn blowing. Skinny turned to his wife.
"That damn Loyd Duncan headed out someplace again!"
She looked at the truck as it raced by.
"He really ought to settle down with some good woman."
Their young daughter perked up.
"Where's his wolf??"
Skinny pulled on out to the highway.

"I heard he run off to the woods a few
weeks back and never returned. Poor
fellow. Him and that big black monster
were like one. Say, who wants a Tasty
Freeze ice cream?!"
Their daughter clapped and hollered.
"Me!! Me!"
Skinny's wife smiled.
"Me too."
They headed toward Hartford.

Junior walked back to the truck. They ate
and Butch climbed into the floorboard,
made three circles, then laid down. Junior
slumped in the seat with his pillow and
soon they both fell asleep.

28

The next morning at 6:30, Skinny opened the doors to the produce stand. He sat three cat head biscuits and country ham wrapped in tin foil along with two small bowls of red-eye gravy on the counter. He also had a large Thermos of coffee and a couple of cups. Junior sat up in the truck seat when he heard the doors open. Butch was already out in the parking lot looking for the perfect spot to do his business.
"Morning!!" Junior called out.
"Come on in! You can use the bathroom in the stand to freshen up. The wife made us breakfast."

Junior was kind of thinking the gravy may be the best thing he had ever tasted while Butch downed his biscuit in two bites.
"You live here in Slocomb, Skinny?"
Junior couldn't completely get his mind away from the ham and biscuit but he was curious.

"Nah. I live up the road in Hartford. I
peanut farm and got a good-sized garden
that stocks the stand. Except for the
tomatoes and I get them here in Slocomb.
Been there most of my life. I served a few
years in 'Nam, got married and moved here
from Dothan when I was twenty-two. The
wife's from here. We've been here ever
since. Can't think of anywhere else I
would want to be. Well every now and
then, maybe Jamaica when I'm alone and
had a few beers, but that don't last."
Junior finished the last of his biscuit
wishing he had three more.
"You like it that good. Dang. You think
there is any room left for a stranger from
Daleville?"
Skinny laughed.
"Heck yes, always. The old McInnis place
is up for sale. Might be just right for you.
Two bedroom, one bath, kitchen and living
room with a nice front porch on fifteen
acres. Mary, the daughter is tired of
messing with it and probably would sell it
right."

"Sounds good, but fifteen acres wouldn't make much of a farm."

"Old man McInnis didn't exactly farm. He did grow some corn and sugar cane. He became richer than Uncle Sam farming a different kind of produce, all squeezed up in a jar. Rumor has it the still rests in one piece in the woods behind his place. He passed last year at the ripe old age of 92. Folks say he worked right up to the last day."

This set Junior thinking.

Skinny refilled their coffee cups.

Junior took a sip.

"So you're completely sold on this place?"

Skinny put the top back on the empty Thermos.

"I'll give you five reasons. It's in south Alabama and that should be enough. The women are all beautiful, loyal, honest. They can all cook and are mostly barefoot. Some barefoot *and* pregnant. The children all have chores, they study hard, play hard and they have respect. The town folk all get along every day of the year except for one. The Auburn - Alabama game. We come close to blows after the game, but then it's over. We laugh, have another beer and start out talking about next year."

Skinny took the Thermos and walked to his truck. He threw it in the front seat and picked up two large baskets of produce from the back. Refills for the stand.

Junior looked over at him as he sat the baskets on the counter. He threw the wadded-up tin foil in the can by the counter.
"I think I'll ride over to Hartford and check on the McInnis place. I'll stop back when I'm headed out of town."
Skinny nodded and went about filling up the baskets. Junior called for Butch and he came running. They both got in the truck.

Junior sat there for a minute. He thought about JW and hoped he was doing okay at

the beach. Later he would find out that he
was inspired by the Gulf and went on a
songwriting spree. He would hook up with
a little band from Alabama called Wild
Country, playing at the Playhouse Lounge.
They would change their name and have a
string of hits a mile long.
Junior thought about Sylvia and realized
she wasn't that far from here. This McInnis
place might be the ticket.

He opened the truck door before he cranked
it and stood on the running board. Skinny
stopped what he was doing and turned
around as Junior called out.
"Wait a minute! That's only four reasons.."
Skinny looked back at Junior with the eyes
of wisdom of a much older man.

"You're only seven minutes away from a
Slocomb tomato."

<div align="center">~~~~~~~~~~~~~</div>

119

Just in case you wanted to know.
Junior bought the McInnis property. He
paid cash for the place.
No, he didn't make moonshine, at least
that's what folks thought. He found he
enjoyed helping Skinny at the produce
stand on weekends.
Sylvia made a visit most every Monday and
stayed a couple days. Junior bought her an
old Oldsmobile Cutlass to make the trip. A
green one, with a little rust.

Butch loved the new home and settled in
before Junior. A year passed and Skinny
gave Junior one of his new pups. A flop-
eared who-knows-what. Junior named him
Butch Junior but called him BJ. Sylvia
giggled every time Junior referred to him.

The Choctaw built a casino on the Daleville
land. Sixteen story hotel, a large gambling
area with a steakhouse restaurant, buffet
and a gift shop. It even had a branch of the

Daleville Bank inside. They let the Georgia pines stay.

Glenda Wells became the hostess at Ruth's Chris Steakhouse. She was fired after a year when she was caught stealing tips.

JW moved to Nashville and became part of the big life. He even started wearing clothes. Later he moved back to the beach where he was most happy. He watched the sunsets and Junior let him stay in the townhouse for nothing.

Miss Bevel stopped smoking and drinking. She passed away a few weeks later. Junior kept the townhouses and they stayed rented year around.

Wilbur got the contract to keep up the casino buses. He build a huge house and became a big deal. A week after Junior purchased the McInnis place Wilbur showed up pulling Junior's old tractor with his tow truck. Junior almost cried, but

instead, he and Wilbur put away a case of
beer. Wilbur had to stay overnight.

Bob the Mailman stayed Bob the Mailman.
Only with a lot more mail to deliver.

Lloyd Duncan made it from Geneva,
Alabama to Alaska, but that's a whole other
story……

There be bears in Alaska.

**The secret of life is enjoying
the passage of time.**

James Taylor

About the Author

Originally from Dothan, AL and now residing in Panama City, FL, Tommy retired after having a stroke a few years back. As he was recovering, he was able to pick up where he left off: Coming up with fun and inspiring stories and books for Facebook friends and anyone who likes to read.

t32408@yahoo.com

Have you read Lloyd?
Available at Amazon and all major booksellers.